WET DREAMS ON LOCKDOWN

Lieutenant Grace

PREQUEL TO "BOUND TO A SAVAGE"

P. WISE

URBAN AINT DEAD

URBAN AINT DEAD
P.O Box 448
Maybrook, NY 12543

Copyright © 2024 By P. Wise

All rights reserved. Published by URBAN AINT DEAD Publications.

Cover Design: P. Wise / The Wise Services

Edited By: Artessa Michele-Thomas / Editing01

URBAN AINT DEAD and coinciding logo(s) are registered properties.

Contact Author on FB: Authoress P. Wise/ IG: @ceo.pwise/ Email: Author.p.wise@gmail.com

Contact Publisher at www.urbanaintdead.com

Email: urbanaintdead@gmail.com

ISBN: 979-8-9888415-9-3

CONTENTS

Facebook Group: <u>Words of the Wise (P. Wise Book Group)</u>

P.O Box 923

Brookhaven, PA 19015

SOUNDTRACKS

Scan the QR Code below to listen to the Soundtracks/Singles of some of your favorite U.A.D titles:

Don't have Spotify or Apple Music?
No Sweat!
Visit your choice streaming platform and search URBAN AINT DEAD.

Currently on lock serving a bid?
JPay, iHeartRadio, WHATEVER!
We got you covered.

Simply log into your facility's kiosk or tablet, go to music and
search URBAN AINT DEAD.

URBAN AINT DEAD

Like & Follow us on social media:
FB - URBAN AINT DEAD
IG: @urbanaintdead
Tik Tok - @urbanaintdead

SUBMISSIONS

Submit the first three chapters of your completed manuscript to urbanaintdead@gmail.com, subject line: Your book's title. The manuscript must be in a .doc file and sent as an attachment. The document should be in Times New Roman, double-spaced, and in size 12 font. Also, provide your synopsis and full contact information. If sending multiple submissions, they must each be in a separate email. Have a story but no way to submit it electronically? You can still submit to URBAN AINT DEAD. Send in the first three chapters, written or typed, of your completed manuscript to:

URBAN AINT DEAD
P.O Box 448
Maybrook, NY 12543

DO NOT send original manuscript. Must be a duplicate.
Provide your synopsis and a cover letter containing your full contact information.
Thanks for considering URBAN AINT DEAD.

Prologue

"Tiffany, relax," my friend, Angela, told me.

It was easier said than done. My legs were shaking uncontrollably as I felt heat flashes run throughout my body. I sat on the couch waiting for the result to appear on the pregnancy test.

"Now, you know her anxiety level is at its all-time high right now," my other friend, Shanay, chimed in.

Angela and Shanay had been my girls since high school. We have been through hell and back together. It was nothing too tough for us to get through when we had one another by our sides. Taking a pregnancy test to see if I was finally pregnant again, was just another experience we were doing as one.

"Can someone go check the shit already?" I snapped, jumping up from my seat.

Both ladies looked at each other before looking at me. They slowly got up and walked to the bathroom that was adjacent to Shanay's master bedroom. Moments later, they walked back out with straight faces, as Angela held the test in her hand.

"So, what does it say?" I asked, biting my bottom lip.

Angela handed the test over to me and, once I saw it was positive, tears started to flow almost immediately.

"Congratulations Tiff," Shanay stated with excitement.

"Congrats, baby," Angela added.

My boyfriend of three years, Richard, and I were trying to get pregnant. After many attempts, we went to see a doctor. Tests were ran, and everything came back normal. The doctor told us we were both healthy and we just had to stay patient and consistent with things.

"I can't believe it," I cried softly. The girls rushed over and hugged me tightly. I couldn't wait to get home to Rich to give him the great news.

"Let me guess, you finna cut our girls' night short and go home to yo man?" Shanay asked, sarcastically.

"Shit, I would've done the same thing. Fuck y'all hoes," Angela joked, making everyone laugh.

I happily gathered my things and rushed out of my girl's house. Hopping in my whip, I started up my car and pulled off with the destination as home.

HURRIEDLY PULLING ONTO MY BLOCK, I saw a parking spot and fit right in. I noticed Rich's car was still there, which told me he was still home. Jumping out of the car, I grabbed my purse and made my way to the front door. I was so excited, I started to fumble the keys in my hands.

Although I was excited to share the news with Rich, I was also nervous. Things between us became rough, and we just weren't seeing eye to eye. I knew he was out cheating, so I prayed the baby would bring us closer.

Finally finding my bearings, I unlocked the door and crossed the threshold. Slipping off my Uggs, I looked around the quiet place. The only thing that could've been heard was the TV in our bedroom. I thought he must've fallen asleep while watching a movie.

Making my way upstairs to our room, I opened the door to find my man and another woman cuddled up naked in our bed. The emotions I felt were indescribable. I was unable to move, think, or even feel at that moment. My body stiffened up as I felt my heartbeat pause for a moment. I didn't know what to do as I watched him hold her close while she laid her head on his chest, a place I used to lay.

I thought about just walking out of the room quietly as if I didn't see anything. Then, I had other thoughts of going to get a knife and stabbing both of their asses up. Conflicted on what to do, I finally went and got Rich's gun from one of his hiding spots. He had guns laid all around the house for emergencies and, at that time, I had an emergency.

I checked the clip and cocked the Glock back. Walking back into the room, they both were still sound asleep, so I crept over to his side of the bed and stood over him. Aiming the gun at his head, I tapped his forehead a few times to wake up him. When he finally opened his eyes, he looked bewildered and sat up quickly, pushing the woman to the side.

"Tiffany," he gasped.

I shoved the gun back into his forehead. His side bitch woke up to the scene and started to scream until I pointed the gun at her.

"Bitch, shut the fuck up," I gritted through clenched teeth.

She quieted down immediately as she shielded her trembling naked body with the covers.

"So, this is what we're doing?" I returned my attention to Rich.

"Baby, I can explain." He raised his hands.

"Baby? Richard, I thought you said y'all were done?" the woman asked.

Both our eyes burned a hole through him, as he fumbled to get a word out. The strong, handsome, aggressive man I knew always to have an answer seemed small and weak while the barrel of the gun stared him down.

I pulled the pregnancy test out of the back of my jeans with my free hand and threw it at him. He looked at the test with a blank expression, only making me angrier.

"Fuckin' dickhead," I scoffed, lowering the gun for a second.

Rich saw the opportunity and rushed me to the ground, as we fought for the gun. Once he gained the upper hand and had possession, he pistol-whipped me as if I was a nigga on the streets.

"Stupid bitch," he growled.

"Please, the baby," I pleaded.

He stood to his feet and hovered over me with malice in his eyes. "Fuck you and that baby."

He started to kick me in my stomach and stomp me out. I curled up in a fetal position, trying my best to save my unborn child. After about a minute of constant hits and kicks, he stopped and left the room. Surprisingly, the woman rushed over to my aid, and as I tried to get up, I felt a wave of nausea. My body felt off and my stomach started to cramp uncontrollably, giving me hints that everything wasn't alright.

Rich left the woman and me in the house and went about his business. I called up my girls, who rushed over and got me to the emergency room. When it was all said and done, I lost my baby and my man on the same night.

A year later…

"Tiff!" Rich hollered from downstairs.

I was curled up in my bed relaxing when I heard his voice travel through the house. Whenever I heard him call for me, I felt a sense of annoyance.

There I was, still with the same man who kicked my child out of my stomach after I found him and another woman in my bed. After some time apart, he came back begging and pleading. I took him back, only because he manned up and finally proposed to me.

Many people told me I was dumb and stupid of course, but at the end of the day, it was up to me. I loved Richard with all of me. We met while I was working as a Lieutenant in a prison where he was incarcerated. Once we became serious, I resigned and waited for him to be released to start our life.

Things were great in the beginning, but what new relationship wasn't? We loved on each other, fucked like rabbits, and planned a whole life with one another. Rich was all I saw, that was until I saw another side of him time and time again.

"Tiffany, you don't hear me calling you?" he yelled even louder.

Flinging the covers off my body, I swung my legs out of the bed and made my way out the bedroom and down the stairs. Rich was on the game playing Call of Duty like he usually did when he was inside, which was once in a blue moon; he loved to run the streets.

"Yes." I stood next to the TV with my hands on my hips.

He glanced at me for a second, not trying to take his eyes off the game. "Come suck my dick," he demanded.

While I wanted to sigh out loud and refuse, I knew I would've felt his wrath if I did. He became not only super abusive, but his words used to cut deeper than the hits. Besides, we weren't having much sex, so that was the most action I was getting in a while.

Walking over to him, I dropped to my knees and pulled his dick out of his pants while he continued to play the game. I had to block out the cursing and carrying on he was doing with whoever it was he was in a match with. It wasn't the ideal moment or mood for what he wanted, but I still did it.

Try doing something you usually loved to do but couldn't

enjoy it. It was one of the worst feelings. I had a high sex drive, and Rich knew that. So, when he started to not please me in the manner he used to or should've, I knew it had to be someone else in the picture.

After a few minutes of getting Rich off, I found myself back upstairs to brush my teeth and freshen up. It was a Saturday evening, and I felt the urge to go meet up with my girls. Once I shot everyone a text in the group chat, not long after, everyone replied and agreed to a girls night. Not wasting a second, I dashed into action and got myself ready for the night.

"So, wait, you're telling me you haven't gotten any dick in how long?" Shanay quizzed with her face scrunched up.

"Three—"

"Three what? I hope days," Angela jumped in.

"Months," I spoke lowly in embarrassment.

"Oh, fuck no. That's way too long, especially for someone who's married," Shanay exclaimed.

Who the fuck you telling? I thought to myself. Listening to my girls take turns expressing their frustration for me only made me more upset. I was unhappy, and the only thing that was keeping me from leaving or doing anything was the piece of paper that bound us.

I was raised in a two-parent household and was used to

seeing all the couples in my family stick shit out until the grave. Automatically, I felt I had to do the same since I took that vow.

"Tiffany, I hate this for you," Angela voiced.

I looked up at my friends and saw how hurt they were as if it was them going through it. "I hate this for me too," I added.

There was no doubt in my soul that I was in a fucked-up predicament. Not only was I unhappy and sexually frustrated, but I was losing my mind as the days went on. All I did was stay home and be a housewife, cooking, cleaning, and sucking dick here and there. I worked nowhere since Rich didn't want me to. Once he was released from prison, he got right back in the streets, but that time, he moved smarter and didn't exactly get his hands dirty.

"What we're not gon' do is have a pity show. You need to boss up and get back to the Tiffany we know," Shanay suggested.

"She's right. For starters, you need to start back earning your own coins. Get the fuck out of that house and get some fresh air. Who knows, you just might run into something that'll get your mind off your boring ass life," Angela chimed in.

"I haven't worked in a hot minute, whew." I leaned back in my seat as I took a sip of the wine we were drinking.

Just the thought of working again made me excited. If I went back into the correctional field, I knew I would have countless action to keep me on my toes. Working in a prison or jail was a world of its own and very entertaining.

"I don't think that's a bad idea actually," I spoke up.

"My job is hiring, I can get you pulled in asap. Plus, with your credentials and experience, they'll be begging for you to start tomorrow," Angela stated.

Angela worked at the Federal Detention Center in Philadelphia. She wasn't a correctional officer, but she held a high position in the building as the Warden's secretary.

"You think so?" I raised a brow.

"Girl, yes. I'm finna shoot my boss a text now and the Captain."

I quickly sunk into my thoughts on how things would be if I went back out to work. Money wasn't an issue when it came to Rich, but I also didn't go anywhere or do anything to need a large amount. Working was more so for a sense of independence and a distraction from my reality.

"Rich ain't gon' like this, but you know what, fuck it. Send the text."

The girls squealed out in excitement as we all raised our glasses in the air. For once, I felt like I was doing something for myself.

"To our girl getting back her life," Shanay stated.

We touched glasses and took a sip.

Yeah, to me getting back my life, I said to myself.

Angela got on her phone and texted who she had to text right away. We all continued to drink and talk for the remainder of the night. By my last drink, I forgot I had to go back home to Rich and my dull-ass life.

As I was getting ready to head to my interview, which Angela got set up the very next Monday, Rich was asking me a million questions.

"Out of all the jobs in the world, why you have to go back into a prison?" he huffed.

I calmly applied my make-up lightly while he went on a rant saying and asking all kinds of shit. The insecure side showed. He wouldn't have anything to worry about if he was taking care of home entirely.

"Rich, please. The opportunity presented itself, so I'm going to take it. I'm tired of being home doing nothing but cooking, cleaning, and being your wife. I need to get active again," I explained, but my words went through one ear and out the other.

"I ain't tryna hear none of that shit. Why yo ass couldn't go be a damn postal worker or some shit? They real active, the fuck. Matter of fact, if you go through with this job shit, you gon' start paying half of everything in this bitch."

Spinning around on my stool, I faced him with a blank expression on my face. "Anything else?" I cocked my head to the side.

Rich thought he was doing something by telling me I had to start helping with the bills. If only he knew, I would be more than happy to do so. And he knew good and well I was going to be able to pay for everything in full by myself. I just prayed my new attitude got his straight because he was losing me, little by little.

"Keep playing with me, Tiffany." He wagged his finger in my direction and stormed out of the room.

Once he was gone, I politely turned back around and continued to get myself ready. My interview was in an hour and a half, and I didn't want to be late.

ARRIVING IN THE CITY, I checked the time and saw I was twenty minutes early. I easily found parking on the street on the same block as the detention center. Climbing out of my car, I looked up at the massive gray building with tiny slit windows you couldn't see in. I took in the scenery of my potential workplace. I was used to being in a compound like a prison with a tall, doubled fence and bob wires all around the perimeter.

Walking around to the front of the building, there was a line of people waiting to get in. Observing the crowd as I walked up to the entrance, it looked like it was family members waiting to visit their loved ones. I excused myself and entered inside a full waiting room. Making my way to the front desk, two young female COs were sitting behind it speaking with people.

The line to get to them was long, and of course, it didn't make sense for me to get in it, seeing as though my reason for being there wasn't the same as others.

"Excuse me for a moment, please? I'm not visiting," I told the woman who was in the front of the line. Surprisingly, she didn't give me a hard time; she allowed me to go in front of her.

"It's no skipping, so wait your turn," one of the COs turned her lip up and said.

"I have an interview in less than fifteen minutes with the captain. Do you still need me to go to the back of the line?" I asked sarcastically.

"Oh, I'm sorry. I'll let him know you're here."

I shot her a faint smile as I stepped to the side while she made the phone call. Moments later, she told me he was aware that I had arrived, and someone would take me to him shortly. Instead of sitting, I just stood to survey my surroundings and take note of how things were done.

"Mrs. Grace?" I heard a familiar voice call out to me.

When I turned in the direction where I heard my name, I saw who the person was. *Get the fuck out of here*, I thought.

When I locked eyes with my old fling, Curt, I felt a wave of nervousness run throughout my body. By the expression on his face, he was just as surprised as I was.

"Tiff? What you doing here?" he asked as we approached each other.

"I have an interview. I would ask you the same thing, but the answer is obvious," I retorted.

He smiled and nodded his head, then motioned for me to follow him. The huge steel gate was opened for us to enter; then, we walked to the elevators.

"Last we spoke, you were at the jail in Delaware County," he blurted out.

"And last I checked; you weren't even into corrections."

We both looked at each other for a second and started laughing as we got onto the elevator. Curtis was one fine ass man. He stood about six feet, a solid football player kind of build, dark-skinned, and had a full goatee that I loved to tug on when we fucked. We had some of the best sex. When I noticed Rich and I were getting serious, I slowly allowed things to fade between Curt and me. We didn't leave on bad terms or anything, the fling just ended.

"Yeah, I had an opportunity and took it. Been here ever since," he explained. "What position are you here for if you don't mind me asking?"

"I'm not even sure. My girl hooked this up and just told me to show up."

"Ah, okay. I see. I wouldn't have known it was you with that last name. Married now?"

Just as I was about to open my mouth to speak, we came to a stop and the doors opened, prompting us to walk off the elevator. I continued to follow him throughout the halls where I saw COs and some male inmates being escorted to different places.

Finally, to what I assumed to be the captain's office, Curt knocked on the door before entering while I waited to be called in. Seconds later, he opened the door wide and motioned for me to come inside.

"Thanks, Lee," a Caucasian man sitting behind a desk told Curt, addressing him by his last name.

Curt walked past me, and when his body brushed against mine, I felt an electric wave rush throughout my body.

"I'll see you later," he spoke softly as he walked out.

In my head, my thoughts were, if I got the job, I already saw that it would be some shit happening with Curt and myself.

Reverting my attention to the captain, I walked up to him and shook his hand firmly.

"Mrs. Grace, I'm glad you could make it so soon. I'm Captain Turner. Please, have a seat," he introduced himself.

As soon as I sat down, we jumped right into things. At first glance, he seemed to be a hard ass, which I expected because of his position and line of work, but one on one, he was very pleasant, respectful, and cool. We ran down my credentials and experience. After speaking about certain facilities, we found we shared in common some old co-workers. Overall, the interview went great, and he told me he was going to meet with the warden immediately after, so to expect a call.

On my way out of the building, I ran into Curt, who was on his break. The way he looked at me made me feel warm in between my legs while all sorts of wild things invaded my thoughts.

"How did it go?" he asked with a smirk.

"Great. So, we'll see."

"That's wassup. Where you park?"

I pointed down the block in the direction of my car.

"Come on, I'll walk you," he offered.

We walked and had small talk along the way. Once we reached it, he just kept staring down at me as if I was a meal he was trying to devour.

"Take my number, but only if your husband won't be drawin."

"You thought you were slick. I like how you fit that in there. And yes, I'm married," I confirmed.

"That's cool." He took my phone, which was already open, and saved his contact information.

I took my phone back and went ahead and unlocked my car door. As I was getting in, Curt pulled me by the arm and wrapped his around my body, giving me a tight hug that made me want to melt.

"Make sure and use my number," he mentioned before planting a kiss on my forehead like he always did.

My words got stuck in my throat, so I just nodded and smiled. He walked away back down the block while I got in my car with a million things on my mind. The attention felt good, and not one part of me felt guilty about wanting it.

Ring! Ring!

My phone started to go off, but I didn't recognize the number.

"Hello?" I answered.

"Mrs. Grace, it's Captain Turner," he revealed.

"Oh, hi."

"I'm calling with good news. You're hired, but not as a regular corrections officer. We'd like to bring you in as my head lieutenant. How does that sound?"

"What? Seriously?"

"Very serious," he stated.

"I'd love that," I beamed.

All I wanted was to get back to work, but starting high in the ranks like I never left the field was a blessing.

"I'll have HR send over everything. We'll see you soon."

"Yes, sir. Thank you so much."

We hung up, and I couldn't fight the feeling that a lot of things were about to change, and I couldn't wait.

Chapter 2

"I knew yo ass would be back," Curt growled in my ear.

I felt myself coming again, creaming all over his dick. Curt bent me over to touch my toes as he gripped my waist tightly, so I didn't fall over from the force of back shots he was delivering. The way he had access to the inside of me, he took full advantage and hit my spot every single time he thrust in me.

The feeling of a dick inside me after going so long without getting any had me on cloud nine. I was yearning so badly for some inches to satisfy my sexual urges and not just down my throat.

"Tell me you missed me," he whispered.

"I missed you, baby," I cooed, throwing my ass back.

My back was arched deeply while he tugged on my pony-

tail and gripped my waist with his other hand. I lifted my leg on the chair, giving him more access to dig deeper. Curt's dick filled me up just the way I needed it to. With every stroke, I felt wetter and wetter. Finally, I was reaching my climax.

"Fuck, I'm about to cum," he huffed, speeding up his pace.

"Fuck me deeper," I cried, using my hands to slam his body against mine. "Don't stop."

Ding!

My phone alerted me I had a text message, pulling me straight from my trance.

> Curt: If shit was solid with you and your nigga, you wouldn't have ever hit my line. So, you can miss me with that shit.

You're right, I thought but didn't let him know that. That same day I reconnected with Curt, I hit his line and we'd been texting back and forth ever since. Our conversations went from catching up to flirting, giving me the very rush I was yearning for. So many nasty and good memories came flooding through my head whenever Curt messaged me. Rich didn't pay me any mind, so I was free to speak to Curt as if he wasn't even around.

It had been a week since the interview and I'd been in constant contact with HR, filling out paperwork and getting ready for orientation and training. For a second, I thought they were going to revoke their offer after my background check came back. Of course, I was clean, but who I was married to came up and I was questioned about his criminal history. After convincing my rep Rich had changed, she got off the topic and continued with the hiring process.

Curt: Anyway, ready for your first day?

That day I had orientation and was scheduled to shadow Captain Turner.

Me: I am. You have work?

Curt: Yeah, I'm heading in now. I'll see you around.

Me: Okay.

I heard the front door open and close, along with the house alarm sounding. Quickly zipping up my duffle bag with my work clothes and things in it, I grabbed my phone and keys to head out of the room. When I made it downstairs, I saw Rich's face buried in his phone as he sat on the couch with his foot up on the center table in the living room.

"Where you going?" he quizzed.

"To work," I simply answered.

Although I knew I got the job not long after I left the interview, I didn't tell Rich. It wasn't like he was excited for me or even cared if I got it or not.

"You ain't tell me you got a job? Where is it? I hope not at FDC." He sat up in his seat.

I rested my bag on the ground, so I could put my sneakers on and tie them.

"So, now you can't hear a nigga talking?" he pushed.

"It's at FDC, Richard." I looked at him blankly.

"Why I'm just now knowing, Tiffany?" He stood to his feet.

I quickly grabbed my bag and unlocked the front door. Rich was sometimes unpredictable, and I wasn't in the mood to be his punching bag that day. Anytime he saw I had some kind of strength; he'd feel intimidated and lash out at me. At that moment, I knew he felt like he was losing control, which he was. I was tired of feeling alone, useless, unwanted, and hurt. But, most of all, I was tired of him.

"Rich, you knew I was going on the interview, and you should know I was more than qualified for the job," I spoke.

"That shit doesn't mean nothing. You ain't tell me you got hired."

"I can't do this right now. I don't want to be late. Lunch and dinner are in the oven." I opened the door and left the house.

As soon as the door closed behind me, I let out the deep breath I didn't notice I was holding in. I swiftly made my way to my car, got in, started it up, and headed to Arch Street.

WHEN I ARRIVED at FDC Philly, the same females were sitting behind the front desk. That time, they were laughing and joking since no one was in the building like the last time. I approached them, hoping to not get the same attitude as the time before, and since I was their superior, it was in their best interest to get their shit right.

"Good morning, ladies," I greeted.

They both looked at me dumbfounded, but the same one who I dealt with quickly recognized me.

"Oh, you were here sometime last week for Captain Turner, right?" she asked.

"Yes, that was me. Can you please let him know I'm here?" I asked of her.

"I got you." She hopped right on the phone and called upstairs to his office.

While she was getting through to him, the other female kept staring at me. I knew I looked good, but it wasn't an admiration stare; it was an envious one. Most people told me I resembled Stacey Dash with a body like Lisa Raye McCoy. I was always an attractive person, so growing up, I had to deal with the hate from women just because of it.

"I'll take you up," the girl spoke after hanging up the phone.

"Okay, cool. Thanks, hun."

I followed her through all the security checkpoints and onto the elevator to the second floor. When we reached Captain Turner's office, she knocked and waited for him to answer, but there was none. Seconds later, he came around the corner talking to a lieutenant.

"Grace, you made it," he spoke with a smile.

"I did." I smiled back.

"Meet your new GS-11 Lieutenant," Turner announced to the CO and lieutenant that was with him. "You will now report to her before you come to me."

A Lieutenant GS-11 was the head lieutenant right under the Captain. We supervised the correctional officers, including the other lieutenants.

The look on the girl's face showed a wave of surprise, and it only gave me a burst of joy inside. It was the very reason you should always act a certain way when people you didn't know were around. You never knew who the person was.

"Nice to meet you guys," I said sweetly.

Turner quickly wrapped up his conversation with the lieutenant, and then led me into his office. We sat and went over a ton of things. I was shown where to change and take my photo for my ID, amongst other things.

The day was spent on the go with Turner while there were times I sat back and did some training on the computer. I met a lot of people, most of whom I forgot their names the moment it was told to me. We frequented some of the housing units and, of course, all eyes were on me. No matter what I had on, my figure and my voluptuous ass couldn't be hidden.

After Turner's time with me for the day came to an end, I was partnered with CO Hunter. She was African American and seemed to have been around my age. I was thirty-seven at the time but still looked like I was in my mid-twenties. By quick observation, she was hip and definitely street, unlike some of the other COs I met who gave off that they were green with many things.

"How long have you been working here?" I asked.

We were on the elevator making our way up to the women's unit for a walkthrough.

"Three years. How long have you been doing this? I know you gotta have some time in since you came right in as our boss," she chuckled.

"I've been in the field for more than ten years," I revealed.

"Makes sense." She nodded.

Once we reached the third floor, we got off the elevator and walked through a steel door, reaching the unit. She rang the bell and asked for my key to open the door. Because of my title, I had full access to almost everywhere in the building except for my superiors' offices. Once open, we walked inside and made our way around the unit.

The ladies were either watching TV, lounging around talking, playing card games, cooking, or eating, while there were some in their cells just chilling. As we walked around, I noticed a good number of them were talking through the toilet bowl, to whom I assumed to be the guys upstairs.

The jails I'd worked in, I never saw that before because the toilet lines weren't set up for it to happen. Plus, the men would only have been able to talk to the men and vice versa.

At FDC Philly, the women were the bottom unit, and five floors up were men on all of their lines, giving the ladies all sorts of options of men to choose from.

I noticed Hunter didn't get on the girls about talking in the bowl, so I questioned it. In the rule book, it was prohibited, but in an environment like that, rules were made to be broken.

"You don't write them up for being on the bowl?" I inquired.

"Nah, for what? They're already in hell. That's the most entertainment they get. But if you want us to crack down on it, then I guess we'll have to," she quickly switched her tone.

"I guess it's something I'd have to observe for myself," I answered honestly.

Usually, we'd allow inmates to do certain things even if it was against the rules if it was something that kept them out of trouble and out of the way. If the act caused a lot of drama and attention to the higher ups, then obviously, it had to be handled.

"Fair enough," Hunter stated with a smirk.

We continued to make our rounds through all the units. Once my day was coming to an end, I found myself in the staff lunch lounge. I was only making myself some coffee to keep me going until I reached home. Just when I was leaving, Curt was walking in. My heart immediately dropped to my stomach.

"Okayyy, white shirt," he sang, walking up to me.

I sipped my coffee and rolled my eyes. Curt was always a

clown and joking every chance he got. Another reason I missed his company, besides the sex.

"Stop it," I told him with a light giggle.

"You really want me to? Lieutenant?" He closed the space between us.

There was no one else in the room but us two, giving him all the opportunity he needed to make his move.

"Do you?" he asked again, touching the small of my back.

I felt the hair on the back of my neck stand up at his touch. My breathing picked up as my heart started to race. Curt's breath brushed my ears as he ran his hand up and down my back.

"No," I allowed to escape my mouth, but somehow didn't regret it.

"I thought so. You still get crazy wet?"

Just by his words, I became moist between my legs. It didn't help that I'd been daydreaming about us fucking ever since we reconnected.

Subconsciously, I nodded my head up and down to answer him.

"What if I told you I'm tryna fuck the shit outta you, Tiffany? Would you let me?"

Curt's mid area was up against my shoulder while I felt his growing dick on my right forearm.

"I would say—"

The door opened, and we quickly made space between each other just in time before someone could see us.

"Oh, Lieutenant Grace, right?" a CO questioned.

"Yes, that's me," I answered with a smile.

"I'm Williams. Nice to meet you." He extended his hand for me to shake.

While I extended mine, I watched Curt exit the room but not before he shot me a wink while he bit the bottom of his lip.

"Nice to meet you, Williams. I look forward to getting to know you." I shifted my attention to the more appropriate person.

If I wasn't careful, I would fall right into Curt's trap. But in the back of my mind, I thought maybe I needed to.

ONCE I GOT HOME from work, I showered, whined down, and relaxed myself. I was so exhausted but mainly my feet were on fire from all the standing and walking I did. It was only a matter of time before my body would adjust to things and get back in tune with being active, so I wasn't worried.

Rich wasn't home when I arrived, allowing me to be at peace. I poured myself a glass of wine, opened this book called *Bound to a Savage* by P. Wise, and laid back in bed until I felt tiredness take over.

Ding!

My phone went off. When I looked, it was a text message from Angela.

Ang: How was your first day, boo?

Me: It was great, no complaints. Thank you so much again, Ang, I appreciate you.

Ang: Girl, please. It's nothing you wouldn't have done for me.

Me: True. I'm beat like a mf though. I'm finna take it down. Back at it tomorrow.

Ang: Mmmhmm, I know the drill. Goodnight girl, love you.

Me: Night, love you too.

I took a gulp of the last bit of wine in my glass, closed the book, and locked my phone. Just when I started to get comfortable in my bed, I heard another text message come in.

Curt: What your thick ass over there doing? Thinking about me?

Me: No, but I bet you're thinking about me.

I giggled as I pressed send.

Curt: I can give you something to think about. You just gotta stop playing with me.

Me: Oh yeah? What's that?

Curt: I can show you better than I can tell you.

Me: Mmmhmm.

Curt: Come sit on my face; I'm tryna taste you.

My eyes bucked from my head at the text. I felt my clit throb as I thought of how his tongue would feel against my lady part. I knew he wasn't bluffing either; he was dead ass serious.

Me: Curt, I can't.

Curt: You can't? Or you won't?

I sat there and watched our thread for a few moments, unsure of how to respond. Before I could text back, he sent another message, halting mine.

Curt: *Location*.

Curt: I'll be waiting.

Curiosity got the best of me, so I clicked the location and saw he wasn't far from me. Only fifteen minutes, to be exact.

What to do, what to do? I asked myself as I sat up in my bed. My body was telling me to go while my head was telling me to stay put. I sat there and contemplated on what to do and, after a while, I finally made my mind up.

"I KNEW you wouldn't have been able to resist," Curt boasted as soon as he opened his front door.

"I can turn right around." I fake turned to leave.

He quickly grabbed me inside his apartment, closing and locking his door behind us. We didn't even get a chance to move away from the door before he was all over me. Pressing me against the wall, Curt kissed my lips in a rough but passionate way. Both his hands roamed around my body, making their way under my sweatsuit.

Curt had on nothing but basketball shorts. His toned abs were on display while his dick poked through the thin fabric. Wasting no time, he started to undress me, all while still attacking my lips. He hadn't touched me between my legs, and I was already hot and ready for him. It was the anticipation that had me hornier than ever.

Once my sweats were off, Curt picked me up, wrapped my legs around his waist, and carried me into his bedroom. Lying me on his bed, he slipped my panties off and spread my legs apart. He looked down at me with hooded eyes and a lustful look then descended between my legs and latched onto my pearl, sending me into a complete frenzy.

"Curt," I called out as I held onto his head.

His tongue was doing tricks I didn't know were possible. With every lick, suck, spit, and penetration he was doing with his mouth, I felt a flow coming out of me.

"Shiiittt," I cried out. I hadn't felt that way in so long, it was almost foreign to me.

In one swift motion, Curt grabbed onto my thighs and swung me on top of him, so I was sitting on his face. Being in that position gave me the advantage to do as I pleased. I started to grind in a circular motion, as he devoured me from underneath. I grinded against his face so hard, that I was sure I was suffocating him, but him grabbing me down told me he didn't want me to stop.

Planting both my feet on the bed, I bounced up and down on his tongue as he fucked me with it. He used his thumb to apply pressure to my clit, giving me the perfect feel of foreplay. I felt myself coming and my legs started to shake. Moments later, I came all in his mouth and all over his beard.

"Fuckkk," I moaned out as my body jerked.

Curt didn't wait for me to come down from my climax. He grabbed my waist off his face and positioned my pussy right over his rock-hard dick. The head was at my opening and, as he inched his way into me, I felt a little pain, but it quickly turned into pleasure once he was inside of me.

Grabbing my breasts, he sucked on one and caressed the other while thrusting upward inside me. I held onto his neck as I smashed down on him repeatedly, feeling all of him. After some time, he flipped me on my back without taking his dick out. Spreading my legs and lifting them in the air, he pounced my pussy with no mercy. All I saw was his hips working their way in a sexy ass motion, in and out of me.

"Damn, this pussy is still good as fuck," he groaned.

He swung my left leg over and turned me on all fours with

his dick never leaving my tunnel. With one hand gripping my waist with the other around my neck, Curt dug his way in and out of me. He was punishing my pussy as if I was in the wrong for keeping it away from him.

Curt was a heavy talker, but he always backed his shit up. He gave off big dick energy, and that was exactly what he had. I couldn't get enough of him, and I knew for a fact I was hooked once again.

"I'm about to cum," he growled in a deep baritone.

"Me too," I added.

Moments later, I came all over his dick as he fucked me fast and hard. He pulled out, prompting me to turn around and open my mouth. Curt shot his seeds all over and in my mouth. I sat there and licked it all up.

"Still a nasty one, I see," he smirked.

"Mmmhmm."

I was more than satisfied. My itch was finally scratched, and I had no guilt within me. My husband was also a far-distant memory.

Chapter 3

urt had been fucking me like crazy for weeks since our first encounter. It was like my life had just taken a drastic shift. If I wasn't at work, I was in his bed. We'd sneak looks, feels, and quick moments while at work, but we never went all the way. It was times I would just get wet by seeing him. It was nothing personal either. It was all sex that had me in the head space I was in when it came to him.

Work was great. I was getting the hang of everything and everyone. I had no complaints in my day-to-day operations behind the walls. I demanded respect from everyone, and respect was given. As far as the inmates went, they would try their hand, but once shut down and they noticed I wasn't going for the bullshit, they stopped.

I was back in my element doing correctional work. Most

of the time, I didn't have to deal with inmates. I just had to make sure my COs and lieutenants were doing what they needed to do. It had its moments like any other job where it got overwhelming, but nothing too crazy where I couldn't handle things.

Knock! Knock!

"Come in!" I yelled at the door.

I was in my office looking over some paperwork regarding a recent incident in one of the male units. In walked one of my COs with a stack of paper in her hands.

"More shit?" I quizzed, referring to shots that my officers gave out.

"Yup. And Captain Turner said don't be late for the meeting," she informed me.

My eyes darted to the time on my computer screen, and I saw I had a few minutes before the meeting started. "Thanks."

She left my office, closing the door behind her.

I rested the new set of incident reports in my to-do pile, then grabbed my things to head to the meeting. Leaving out my office, I ran into Curt escorting an inmate.

"Where you off to?" he asked.

"A meeting and you?" I looked at the undeniably handsome inmate.

"Finna take him back to his unit. Find me once you're done," he stated in a flirtatious tone.

"Okay."

During the entire encounter, the inmate just stood there

staring me down, sizing me up. Usually, I would feel uncomfortable because most of the guys were perverts, but it didn't feel that way with him.

He was tall, about six-two since he had a little height over Curt, light-skinned, and had amazing, soul-piercing green eyes that had me captivated. I tried my best to not show that I was checking him out, but the shit was hard. I was just thankful Curt kept the conversation short and sweet.

I swiftly made my way to the meeting, but I couldn't get the image of the inmate out of my mind. It was like déjà vu when Rich and I met, and I knew there was no way I could go down that road again. Although messing around with Curt was still considered dealing with someone from my workplace, he could leave the building when that time came.

The meeting went on for about an hour amongst the department leaders. Since I was right under the captain, I had to be there to represent alongside him. Once the meeting was over, I returned to my office and Curt followed not long after.

"You good?" he asked as he entered my office.

My face was back buried in paperwork so, before I left for the day, they were taken care of.

"Yeah, I'm good. You?" I questioned without taking my eyes off the incident report I had on top.

"Yeah. I need to holla at you about something, though."

"Can it wait?" I looked up to see him pacing the floor.

"I mean it can, but I rather it not."

Resting down the pen on my desk, I leaned back in my desk and watched him. "Wassup Curt?" I quizzed.

He finally halted his movements and took a seat in front of my desk. "Promise me whether you agree to it or not, this doesn't leave this room, nor will you fuck shit up?" he stated with a serious facial expression.

"What is it?" I started to get skeptical.

"Promise me, Tiff."

What the hell, it can't be nothing crazy, I thought.

"Promise." I held my locked index and middle finger together under the desk, out of eyesight.

"The nigga I was with earlier, Manic. He runs shit in here. To be specific, drugs. I work with him, and before you start tripping, it's a lot of money involved. He's that nigga on the streets, Tiff."

I looked at Curt to see if he was serious or if it was some kind of joke, but when I saw he wasn't budging and had a stern look, I knew it was real. "You're dead serious?" I wanted to confirm.

He nodded as he shifted his weight from one side to the next in his seat. I took a deep breath in and let it out as I took in what he just told me.

At my previous job, I would indulge in minor illegal activities like getting in phones, and some cigarettes, but nothing major like what he was implying. I wasn't always the perfect correctional officer; shit, I wasn't always the perfect person. If it was a way to make some extra money and not get caught, why not?

"Run everything down to me, so I can see if it's something I can deal with," I opened up.

A huge grin graced Curt's face as he leaned up and rubbed his hands together.

"Bitch, be humble, sit down, be humble," I heard Angela rapping along to Kendrick Lamar's song, *Humble*, as she entered my office.

I was on a call with one of the unit secretaries, so I held my finger up to silence her. Playfully, she covered her mouth in a childlike manner as she started to look around my office.

"Okay, thanks so much. I'll be looking out for the email," I told the woman on the other line and hung up. "Girl, come in here acting like you got some sense." I snapped my neck at her.

"Sense is something I don't have, you should know that by now," she retorted. "Heyyy, friend."

I couldn't help but laugh. Angela brought the ghetto side out of me, and I never complained. "Wassup, girl? What you doing around these parts with us peasants?"

"Oh, nothing, just checking to see if y'all doing y'all jobs or whatever." She plopped down in the seat in front of me and crossed her legs. "And I wanted to lay eyes on my lil' jawn I have here," she revealed.

"Lil' jawn? You fuckin' someone in here Ang?" My eyes bucked.

She started to giggle like a little girl, giving me my answer.

I guess I ain't the only one then, I thought.

"Shhh, you're all loud." She held her index finger up to her lips. "But, yeah, I have someone around these parts chile."

"Who?" I was so curious.

"I can't tell you," she started to sing.

"Wow, that's how it is now?" I raised a brow.

"Chill, Tiff. Once I know where exactly it's going, maybe I'll reveal him."

It wasn't like she was the only one hiding her fling, so I couldn't even be mad. "Fair enough." I smiled.

I was just happy she was having fun with life. Unlike me, I was playing a dangerous game, and it was about to get even more dangerous doing business with an inmate.

"Let me get back to my office before they notice I'm missing. Let's link this weekend," she suggested.

"Sounds like a plan, my love."

She blew me a kiss before leaving out the door.

My mind quickly went to thinking about everything Curt told me. *Makhi Manic Frost*, I said to myself. *What a name.*

The way they were operating was alright for the moment, but a more secure way to get the drugs in was needed. I started to brainstorm how we could've switched things up to stay undetected.

After I got a boatload of paperwork done, I went on some rounds around the building, making sure to stop at five-south where Manic was housed. When I reached the unit, I rang the bell and used my key to let myself in. The guys eyes grew wide when they saw me enter their space. I went straight to the guard booth to check on the CO on duty.

"LT, wassup?" CO Wright greeted me as I approached him.

"Nothing much, just making my rounds. How's things here?" I asked, looking around the busy unit of men.

"Copacetic."

"Nice."

Unbeknownst to Wright, I was already briefed on several people on Manic's payroll, and he was at the top of the list.

"Come walk with me," I told him. He jumped out of his seat, locked up the booth, and started to lead the way.

Although I made it seem like it was a normal walk-through, my focus was Manic. As we bypassed the cells, I glanced inside most of them, and even though I saw things out of place, I paid no mind.

Finally getting to Manic's cell, I stopped and opened the door. He was on his bottom bunk talking to another inmate. When he saw me, his facial expression didn't give off surprise. He acted normal like he knew I was coming.

"Let me talk to him for a minute," I told the inmate, who looked at Manic for confirmation if to leave or not.

Manic gave him a head nod, and he got up and left the cell. Wright stood outside the cell, giving us space to speak.

"What you here for?" He eyed me.

Those being his first words to ever roll off his tongue to me showed me he was one arrogant muthafucker. For some odd reason, I was turned on.

Manic was fine as fuck, from his looks to how his body was built. He had this aura about him that made it hard not to want to get to know him. He seemed vicious like he wasn't someone to play with. By what I'd read up on him, he had a wicked reputation as one of the most feared people in the Tri-state area.

"I spoke with Lee about your proposition."

"Mmmhmm and?" He watched me with one eyebrow raised.

"We can make some things happen," I gave in.

A slight smirk appeared on his face as he turned and looked down at the floor in front of him. "Why do I feel like there's a but coming?"

"Because it is. Things will have to switch up."

He stood to his feet and took a step towards me. I couldn't help but notice the bulge in his gray basketball shorts. His tool was a nice size, and it wasn't even hard.

"Shorty don't think you finna come in and start barking orders. Shit don't work that way."

I cleared my throat because a lump formed, and I was fighting to swallow. He was making me nervous. "It's not even like that. I just found a better way to get your product in the building. Once you agree, I'll make the move for you," I quickly tried to lighten the conversation.

"And that is?" He took another step closer.

"Dr. Gannon. If it's one person that has a lot of freedom in here, it's him," I suggested.

Manic looked at me intensely for a few moments before starting to pace his cell. "Do it. I don't care about the cost," he stated.

I nodded and turned on my heels to leave his cell.

"Don't fuck this up, Tiffany," he spoke nonchalantly as if we were long-time friends. His words sent chills down my spine because it sounded menacing.

I left out his cell, and then the unit altogether. Returning to my office, I wrapped up my day at work and headed home.

IT WAS another regular day at work. While making my rounds in the visiting room, Curt radioed me on the walkie. We met up at my office not long after. A few days had passed since Manic, and I spoke. I went and visited Dr. Gannon. At first, he was very hesitant and felt uncomfortable about everything, but after some proper persuading and a hefty compensation, he agreed to come on board. Once everything was settled, I got word to Manic to set things in motion.

"What's up?" I asked as soon as Curt walked in the door.

"I need you to get someone off the women's unit for me and bring her down the medical hall," he somewhat gave off a demand.

Cocking my head to the side, I was trying to figure out what the fuck he had going on.

"Who and for what? Why you need me to do it and can't get another female CO?" I rattled off question after question.

He sighed out loud and ran his hands down his face.

"Hello?"

"It's for Manic," he simply answered.

"What you mean it's for Manic? You mean—"

"Yes." He shot me a knowing look.

This shit just gets better and better, I thought.

After contemplating for a little, I gave in and went to get the jawn off the women's unit. Her name was Briana, and I couldn't even lie and say she was ugly; she was beautiful and had a nice body. Looking at her, I could tell what type of females he liked.

Curt instructed me to bring her to the back of medical where there were unoccupied offices and traffic was limited. Once we had both of them in the room together, we left them alone. As I was walking off, Curt called out to me.

"Hold on!"

"What now?" I quizzed.

"Stay here for me. I have to do something real quick. I won't be long," he begged.

Immediately, I thought it was a setup or something. Let me had gotten caught condoning the bullshit Manic had going on, it would've been a wrap for me.

"Make it fast, Curt," I grilled.

He didn't waste any time and rushed off. I leaned up against the wall and just patiently waited for them to do what they were doing and for Curt to return.

After a few moments of silence, moans and groans were heard. Curiosity got the best of me, and I peeped into the window of the office. What I saw made my jaw drop.

Briana was on her knees deep throating Manic, as he gripped a handful of her hair guiding her up and down his dick. He must've felt someone looking at him because he looked up and saw me, then wore a menacing grin on his face. We locked eyes all while Briana sucked and slurped on him.

My body started to get hot as I felt my panties getting wet. Manic had a big dick. I was talking hung like a horse. I was so mesmerized, that I couldn't peel my eyes away from the window.

Manic pulled away from her and motioned for her to stand up. Dropping her tan uniform pants to the ground along with her panties, he picked her up and slid her down slowly on his erect tool.

"Fuckkk," Briana cried softly.

He had her back against the wall while her legs were

wrapped around his waist. Holding her hands above her head with one of his hands, he held onto her with his other hand while thrusting upward inside of her. The pleasure that was plastered on Briana's face spoke a million words.

The way he held her, the way his body moved, the way he fucked her, the way she reacted, it all made me want in; it made me want him. And it didn't help that the entire time he looked me dead in my eyes while he pounced his way in and out of her. Manic was trouble, but everything about him had me ready to risk it all.

Just as I took a step away from the door, a CO walked out of a room down the hall and saw me.

"LT Grace, you good?" he asked, walking towards me.

My heart started to speed up even faster than it was already beating. I knew I couldn't let him get close enough to hear and figure something was going on.

"Yeah, I'm fine. Just needed to stretch my legs, so I'm walking around," I lied.

"Oh, alright then. I was just about to say, nothing much happens back there."

Yeah, that's what you think, I thought.

"Yeah, I see."

"They kept Kaboni Savage back there when he was here," he informed me.

I'd heard stories about Savage throughout the Philly streets and, while it was the wrong time for a history lesson, I was intrigued by the information he gave.

"Oh wow, I had no idea. That's crazy."

"Right. Well, I'll see you later, LT." He walked off in the opposite direction.

I let out the deep breath I was holding in, feeling a sense of relief. Curt came around the corner and made his way towards me.

"Finally, what the fuck?" I grilled.

"My bad, you good though, right?" He observed me.

"Yeah." I waved him off.

Another few minutes had passed and there was a knock on the office door. After the coast was clear, Curt let Manic out of the office, leaving Briana still inside. As they walked past, Manic stopped.

"You might as well have joined," he whispered in my ear, sending chills down my spine.

Curt looked at me with a confused look but brushed it off when Manic motioned for him to walk. I wasn't sure if I had the proper willpower to resist him; it was only a matter of time before I folded.

After a few minutes, I went into the office, got Briana, and escorted her back to the women's unit. I had a stinging, jealous feeling while I was around her as if she was fucking on my man. How things were going to play out, I wasn't sure, but I made a mental note to make sure I came out on top and untouched.

Chapter 4

"*How does this shit feel?*" *Manic growled in my ear.*

"Good, baby," I whimpered.

He had me bent over my desk with my ass cheeks spread apart, giving him all the access he needed, and wanted to dig my back out. Lifting one leg on the desk, he tugged at my hair as he delivered forceful back shots. It felt so good. I just wanted to scream out in pleasure but knew I couldn't.

With his thumb in my ass, he worked his dick in and out of me while he did the same with his thumb. Pulling out, he spit on his tool and down my crack, so it slid to my ass and pussy. The next thing I knew, I felt his head at my asshole trying to inch its way inside.

"Manic," I turned slightly and whispered in a hushed tone.

"Shut up and turn around." He pushed me back onto the desk.

The way Manic demanded things, it turned me on. I was submissive to him and anything he wanted, so I did what he said.

His dick was not small in any way, shape, or form so, when I felt him plunge his way into me, I hollered out in pain.

"Fuckkk!" I screamed with my heart racing.

I looked around and noticed I was in my bed dreaming; it felt so real. Touching between my legs, I discovered that I was wet and feeling horny from what I thought was a heated sex session between Manic and me.

Ever since I saw him fuck Briana, I couldn't get him off my mind. It was more than sex with him, though; he played with my mind and didn't even say much. The way Manic moved and operated excited me on a whole other level.

Ring! Ring!

I grabbed my phone from off the nightstand and saw it was my doctor's office calling. "Hello?" I answered.

"Hi, good morning, Mrs. Grace. I know Mr. Grace told us to only contact him, but we've had so many failed attempts. The doctor just wanted you all to know that all the tests came back normal, but he'd like to keep the ultrasound appointment for today at noon to check on the surrogate and the baby," she informed me.

"Baby?" I whispered, dumbfounded.

Surrogate?

"Huh?" the lady on the line said.

At that point, we were both confused, but it didn't take me long to see what was going on. My emotions ran wild as my ears tingled, and my anxiety shot to the roof. Rich had done the unthinkable and got someone else pregnant.

"Okay, no problem. I will let him know, but can you please shoot him a text to remind him as well?"

"Sure, will do."

"Thank you."

As soon as I hung up, I checked the time, which read ten-forty-three a.m. I jumped out of bed and got myself together, so I didn't miss our surrogate appointment. It was such a coincidence that I got that phone call on my day off. I had all the time I needed to see what the fuck was going on.

An hour later, I arrived at our doctor's office in Germantown. Parking a little way down, I noticed Rich's Benz out front of the office. Climbing out of the car, I made my way to the entrance and inside. The moment I walked in, I saw Rich walking behind a woman to the back where the doctor's office was located.

I quickly followed behind them, giving them enough space to get settled before I barged in. He had the audacity to bring whoever the bitch was to our doctor's office and then had the nerve to pretend she was our surrogate. I couldn't make that shit up; I felt like I was living in a real-life Lifetime movie.

The door to the doctor's office was closed, so I knocked and, when I heard to come in, I did just that. While Rich and his side bitch were surprised to see me, I was just as surprised to see it was the same fucking woman I caught him with a year or so before when he beat our baby out of me.

"Mrs. Grace, nice of you to join us," Doctor Philp stated.

"You piece of shit." I mushed Rich's head real hard.

The jawn jumped out of her seat and held onto her stomach tightly like I was about to hit her. Although she deserved to get her ass dragged, I wasn't into harming innocent, unborn babies. But I made a mental note to see her when she dropped her load.

"Wait, wait, what's going on?" Dr. Philp inquired, looking at everyone in the room.

"Yeah, what's going on, Rich?" I asked with my chest heaving up and down uncontrollably.

"You didn't tell her?" the woman questioned him.

"Mrs. Grace, you didn't know?" Dr. Philp quizzed.

"No, this is news to me. But I have some news for you." I looked at Rich. "I want a divorce."

I turned to leave the office with nothing else to say.

"Good luck, because yo' ass ain't going nowhere," I heard him say over my shoulder.

I didn't understand men. He treated me like shit, showed

no love or affection, and had another woman who was pregnant but wanted to keep me around. It just didn't make sense to me how narcissistic people were.

Waiting until I reached my car and behind my wheel, I broke down and allowed the tears to escape. A waterfall rushed down my face as I felt all the pain and hurt all over again from the night I lost my baby. I blamed myself for everything, especially for staying and marrying his trifling ass after what he'd done. To think I could change a man, I was dead wrong.

Granted, I was cheating and having a little fling with Curt, but that's all it was, just sex. I had no feelings for him. I was not planning a future with him and had no thoughts of having his child. Karma spun the block fast on me, or was it a blessing in disguise?

As I was wiping my tears away, a text came through my phone.

Unknown: The doctor got the package, check in with him.

It was a random number I had never seen before but, by the context of the message, I knew what it was about.

I called up FDC to speak with Captain Turner. It was my off day, but I needed to get in there to make sure everything went smoothly with Dr. Gannon. Plus, I thought it would've been a good distraction from my reality.

"Grace, I was just going to call you," he spoke as soon as he got on the line.

"Really? Why?" I raised a brow.

"I wanted to know if you could cover the night shift tonight. We'll be short and it's a transport of over a hundred guys coming in today."

It was like he read my mind. "Sure, I'll be there soon."

"Do as you please," he stated.

Oh, I will, I thought.

"You're fuckin' lying." Angela's eyes grew wide like golf balls.

I had just finished telling her about the revelation that basically dropped in my lap earlier that day. Detail for detail, I broke it down to her with tears threatening to fall but I held them back.

"Yeah," I spoke softly, still in disbelief.

The moment I clocked in, I called Angela's line and told her to come and see me urgently. She dropped what she was doing and came to my office. She comforted and spoke life into me, just like a friend should've.

"So, what you're going to do now?"

"I'm leaving him. There's nothing else to do."

"Yeah, until he starts to act right for like a month and says all the things you want to hear." She curled her lip.

"Nah, I think it's far past that."

"We'll see."

Knock! Knock!

"Come in!" I yelled.

Wright poked his head in the office. "He said to check on the shipment," he discreetly mentioned.

"Okay, I will." I nodded.

He quickly left, closing the door back.

"What was that about?" Angela pried.

"I'll tell you later. Let me go and handle something," I told her.

We both stood up and embraced one another tightly. I needed that hug badly. Once she left, I locked my office door and made my way over to medical, which was on the same floor I was on.

The regular day was almost over. Four o'clock count was just conducted and cleared, which meant dinner was about to start. There was no one in medical but Dr. Gannon. When I knocked on his door, he answered right away and granted me entry.

"Lieutenant," he greeted.

"Wassup Doc, how did it go?"

"Easy, to say the least. I was on edge, but things played out perfectly," he expressed.

"Well, I'm glad." I smiled.

He went into a closet in his office and unlocked a cabinet, pulling out a medical bag. Carrying it over to the examination table, he unzipped the bag and showed me the contents inside. My eyes bulged; it was the first time I was around so many drugs at once.

"It's phones at the side." He pointed.

I ran my hand over the side of the bag and felt three phones. Pulling them out, I saw they were Android, and one was labeled M.A. It didn't take a rocket scientist to know that the phone was for Manic. I secured it on my person, along with the charger, and placed the other two back in the bag until I was instructed on what to do.

"Okay, I'll go and speak to him. Put this away until I let you know what to do," I advised him.

He nodded and zipped the bag back up, placing it back inside the cabinet and locking it with a key. I left out of his office and returned to mine until things got quiet around the building.

AFTER THE NINE o'clock count was finished and cleared, I made a few rounds to different units, including the special housing unit on the eighth floor. That same night, Wright was on duty in Manic's unit, which worked out perfectly for me. Having some officers on board made things much easier than having to sneak around alone to handle things.

When I got to five-south, I had Wright go and get Manic while I waited in the kitchen area that had a gate pulled down and a door. No one could see us in there, so it made sense for us to do the handoff there. The unit was quiet since it was around one o'clock in the morning. I heard one or two guys talking, and I assumed they were either speaking to their cellmate or on the toilet bowl with a girl.

Not long after, the kitchen door opened and Manic appeared wearing just basketball shorts. His toned chest and abs were on display while I caught a glimpse of his dick imprint through his shorts.

"You got something for me or you called me out to look at my dick?" he asked arrogantly.

"Frost, please." I sucked my teeth.

I unbuttoned my shirt, reached into the side of my bra, and pulled the phone out. Then, I pulled the charger out from the other side. Handing it over to him, he observed the items and nodded his head in approval.

"Good shit, LT. How is everything else looking?"

"It's there. I need the names of your folks, so I can get Dr. Gannon to put them on the callout to get their shit. It's the best way to distribute everything. What do you think?"

"I'm tryna figure out where you have been all my life." He bit his bottom lip and took a few steps forward me.

I swallowed the lump that formed in my throat. Being around Manic made me nervous for different reasons. He was dangerously fine and, of course, his reputation would've had anyone shaken.

"Well, I'm here now, right?" I shot him a faint smile.

At that point, the sexual tension in the room was so thick, I couldn't even keep eye contact with him. As he continued to walk towards me, I stood still and didn't take a step back. It was like my feet were cemented to the ground.

Hovering over me with his tall frame, he looked down at me with his piercing green eyes, then gently ran the back of his hand down my arm. Butterflies invaded my stomach as I started to feel weak.

"I make you nervous or something?" he asked in a low tone.

His breath tickled my nose, making my body shiver.

"Let me go." I tried to sidestep him, but he extended his arm and blocked me.

Grabbing me back in front of him, he wrapped his arm around my waist and used the other hand to lift my face to meet his.

"When I talk to you, you look at me in my eyes, ye mean?" he demanded.

I nodded since I couldn't form the correct words to say.

He moved his hand from my face to my neck and gripped it firmly while looking at me dead in my eyes. I melted under his touch, and it wasn't even all the way sexual. His aggression was sexy as fuck.

"Lieutenant Grace, you tryna cum for me?" he asked in a deep baritone.

"I-I—"

"Yes or no," he cut me off. He slowly tilted his head to the side, still staring at me.

"Yes," I allowed to slip from my lips.

"Mmmhmm, I thought so. Get on them knees," he ordered.

Like a servant, I dropped to my knees as he said without hesitation. It was like I was compelled to do as he said and give him what he wanted.

I pulled down his shorts and boxers, and his semi-erect dick just looked me in the face. Not waiting for another second, I stroked him a few times and placed the head in my mouth, toying with it for a moment. In one swift movement, I swallowed his dick whole, or at least tried to. He had length and girth, and from what I saw between him and Briana, he knew how to work his tool.

I felt him grab the back of my head, as he pushed me down his dick. Having his shit deep throat seemed to have been his thing. While he sat at the back of my throat, I vibrated my throat, and that made him jump.

"Oh shit," he whispered.

I sucked the shit out of his dick for a few more minutes until he finally pulled away. Looking at me lustfully, he motioned for me to turn around. I undid my pants with his help. Next thing I knew, as soon as they dropped to my ankles, he had me bent over and playing with my pussy.

"Damn, yo shit pretty." He palmed my whole cat.

From an angle, I saw him go in his shorts and pull out a

condom. My first thought was he had that shit planned all along, but I didn't even trip. It wasn't like I hadn't been fuckin' him in my mind anyway. He slipped on the condom and, without warning, he arched my back and penetrated me.

"Oh fuck," I whimpered, quickly covering my mouth.

Manic filled and stretched me out without giving me time to properly adjust to his size. I tried to put my hand in between us, but he slapped it away.

"Take this shit, don't run."

Hearing his voice made me open up. I took all the pain that came with the pleasure. That day he was fucking me from behind had me thinking he was about to touch my soul. I felt all of him, every stroke, every twist, and the way he held onto my body only made me cum all over his dick.

"Mmmhmm, wet this shit up," he growled.

"Shittt," I cried.

"I'm finna nut."

I pulled away from him, turned around, and descended to my knees. Snatching the condom off, I wrapped my lips around his dick and sucked until I couldn't. I felt his dick jump and pulsate and then felt a warm stream shot down my throat. I swallowed all that man kids whole and made sure none was left behind.

"Damn." He placed his hand under my chin and caressed it. "You tryna make a nigga fall in love, huh?" He smirked.

I giggled and dropped my head out of shyness. Little did

he know, I was finna throw my pussy at him every chance I got. All I could think about was, why couldn't I have met him before I met Rich? Manic would've made the perfect husband, and since I was getting a divorce, it wasn't too late.

Chapter 5

There I was, legs spread apart and skinned out on my desk with everything on display. What was supposed to be a quick meeting between Manic and I in my office turned into a whole heated fuck session.

Manic took the cup of ice water I had and grabbed an ice cube out of it. Placing it on my clit, I jumped at the coldness it gave. He moved the ice cube in a circular motion, then slipped two fingers inside of my tunnel.

"Mmmm," I moaned and threw my head back in ecstasy.

"You like that shit, don't you?" he asked.

Lifting my head, I smirked at him and nodded my head. That man had me wide open, and it had only been about a week we'd been fucking on each other.

Manic removed the ice from my nob, and when I felt it

enter me, my eyes popped open, along with my mouth. My body shook from the pleasure the coldness brought. He positioned himself between my legs and slid in, with the ice still inside of me. With every deep stroke, the ice hit my spot, sending me into a complete frenzy. It wasn't long before it melted due to me coming.

He held me by the back of my neck while one leg was in the crook of his arm. Drilling in and out of me, I thrust upward, fucking him back. I had to match his energy because that nigga was a whole vibe when it came to laying down the pipe.

Manic moved his waist in a way that had me ready to get on one knee and propose to him. He looked deep into my eyes as he slid in and out at a steady pace. It should've been illegal to fuck someone the way he did.

Out of nowhere, he started to speed up, which let me know he was about to come. I had already come several times since we started. After a good number of deep, fast strokes, he pulled out.

"Come swallow this shit."

I quickly hopped off the desk and squatted in front of him. Slurping his dick, I bobbed up and down until I felt the warm, sweet taste of his cum shooting in my mouth.

"Mmmhmm, get rid of every last one of them."

I sucked him dry and made a popping sound when I finally released his dick. Still erect, he slapped his dick on my lips a few times.

"Now, that's how you drain a nigga."

Knock! Knock!

Both of our heads snapped in the direction of the door. I placed my finger on my lip, as we moved quietly around to get dressed. Wright was standing guard a ways down the hall. It would've looked crazy if he stood right outside the door. Usually when my door was closed, I was not in my office, on break, or handling something very important; otherwise, my door was always open. Once I didn't answer, the person would automatically think I wasn't in.

Just as I predicted, whoever it was slid a paper under the door and kept pushing. I went and grabbed it off the floor, then continued to get dressed. Within another minute, we were both fully clothed.

I opened the door and looked out into the hall. Wright was posted up looking like he was doing something. Once he saw me, he started to make his way towards me. The way my office was positioned, it was located in a blind spot, so the camera never picked it up. I thought how lucky I was.

"Ready?" Wright asked me.

I nodded and stepped aside for him to get Manic. As they were walking out of my office, Curt turned the corner and was headed our way. The guys greeted each other in passing. Manic made sure to turn around and shoot me a look before he disappeared around the corner.

"What was he doing here?" Curt questioned, scrunching up his face. "Let me find out y'all doing shit without me."

"Curt, please." I brushed him off.

He followed me inside the office and closed the door. Walking around my desk, I noticed the condom was on the floor. I quickly kicked it out of sight before he saw it.

"I ain't hear from you all week. What, you and your nigga made back up or something?" He wrapped his arms around me from behind.

Me and my new nigga great was what I wanted to say.

"Whatever. It's not even like that. I've just been busy with a lot," I half lied. I was busy getting dug out by Manic.

"I understand. Make some time for me." He kissed me on my neck. "I'm tryna taste you."

Usually, Curt's words and touch would have me ready to slide down his pole, but it made me cringe for some reason. His speaking about eating me out always made me horny, and the fact that Manic never munched on me and I was beyond head over heels for him told me a lot.

"I'll make time." I slipped out of his grasp. "Let me get these reports done, love."

"Ard. I'll let you get to it."

As I took my seat behind my desk, he left my office, leaving me to catch a breath, one that was needed.

A FEW DAYS had passed since I saw Manic. All I did was think about him and I'd instantly get wet. The effect he had on me was strong but also scary. Rich didn't even have that kind of hold on me. He couldn't even fuck me the way Manic did.

I was sitting at my desk on my computer when the thought of checking his emails crossed my mind. The system we had allowed the officers to check the inmates' emails for anything that shouldn't be going on in them. I wasn't going to be looking for them but more so to get a glimpse of who he spoke to daily, which would tell me who was important to him.

Once I logged on and started checking his messages, there were a lot, but the same three frequented his inbox: his mother, baby mother for his daughter, and Briana. I'd learned about the text app the inmates had that allowed them to text whoever instead of having them as an actual contact in the system. Inmates used it to correspond with one another as well, so I figured that's exactly what he and Briana were doing.

Reading their messages made me feel some kind of way. Jealousy was an understatement. I felt she was going to be in the way of me getting Manic to myself, and I was tired of losing.

I hopped on the phone and called five-south, letting them know I needed to see Manic. Calling one of my COs since Wright was on the women's unit at the time and Curt just didn't need to be around, I sent them to escort Manic to me.

About ten minutes later, the officer returned with Manic.

"Thanks. Give me a minute." I motioned for him to close the door.

"Wassup, shorty? You got news for me or something?" Manic asked as he took a seat.

I looked at him closely to observe his mood. He seemed to have been in a normal head space and not agitated like he would be sometimes.

Clearing my throat, I sat up straight in my seat. "So, we've been fucking around for a few weeks now. We're doing great business together and all. I guess what I'm trying to get at and understand is the dynamics of our situation," I voiced.

"What you mean? We chilling." He squinted.

"Are you single, Makhi?"

"I am, what that got to do with anything?"

"You deal with anyone?"

"What's with the line of questioning, Tiffany? A nigga don't like to be pressed. Fuck is going on?"

"I fuck with you, Makhi, hard. I'm just tryna figure out what you got going on with Briana," I blurted out.

"None of yo business, that's what. You got me fucked up, yo." He stood to his feet. "You're not my bitch, so stop watching face. Know your lane and stay in that muthafucker."

Knock! Knock!

"Let these niggas take me back to the unit," he demanded.

The door swung open, and Curt stood there with an unpleasant face.

"Aye, take me back upstairs," Manic told Curt as he walked past him out the door.

Curt shot me a death stare, then followed behind Manic.

I couldn't believe that things went left so fast. The way we were vibing, I thought we were better than that. In all honesty, I knew we would've been extra solid if the Briana chick wasn't in the picture, so I knew what I needed to do: get rid of her.

About ten minutes later, Curt returned to my office, closing my door shut. He wore a wicked scowl on his face. I never saw him that upset before.

"What's your problem?" I quizzed.

"You fucking that nigga?" he came right out and asked.

"Curt—"

"Answer the question, Tiffany."

Who the hell did he think he was pressing me that way? He wasn't my daddy or my nigga. Curt was just a piece of dick I sat on here and there.

"Yes, I am," I boldly stated.

"Hoe ass bitch," he gritted. "I put you on to make some good ass money and you run off with the plug? Well nah, I'll take that back because he don't even fuck with you like that. He's only using you, dickhead."

"You sound jealous. That's a female trait, Curtis." He started to chuckle.

I couldn't front and say I wasn't hurt by his words. The shit hit me hard, but I kept a poker face.

"Tiffany, you fucked up. That's all I'ma say. Enjoy it while it lasts."

"Excuse me? Is this some kind of threat?" I raised a brow.

"You heard me. You switched up on the wrong nigga. I promise you'll regret everything." He stormed out of my office, leaving me there with all kinds of thoughts running through my head.

I plopped down in my chair and took a couple of deep breaths in and out to calm my nerves. Shit went haywire out of nowhere. I thought I had drama at home with Rich, but things at work took the cake. While I wanted to feel sorry for myself, I just couldn't. I wasn't a weak bitch, and I was tired of people trying to walk all over me.

Picking up my office phone, I dialed Angela.

"Ms. Cummings speaking," she answered on the first ring.

"Ang," I spoke.

"Tiff?"

"Yeah, I need a favor."

"What's up boo?" she asked.

"An inmate just got sentenced and waiting to be designated. Can you speed up the process?"

"What's the name?"

"Briana—"

"Oh, Briana. I know her. She's a little troublemaker but harmless in my eyes."

"Well, yeah, her. Can you make that happen?"

"Yeah. I'll make the call to my connect down at Grand Prairie."

"Thanks, girl, and come by Shanay's tonight. I need a drink or ten."

"Say less, I'll see you later."

LATER THAT NIGHT, I went to my house to grab some more clothes. Ever since I found out about Rich and his side bitch expecting, I gathered some of my things and went to stay at Shanay's spot. There was no way in hell I could've stayed under the same roof as his ass.

He blew up my phone with calls and messages nonstop for weeks until I changed my number. Then, he sent me emails and reached out through social media. He even went as far as to send me messages with money transactions through Cash App. I gladly accepted the money and ignored what he had to say.

Lucky for me, when I reached the house, he wasn't home. I grabbed what I needed and quickly got out of dodge. Shanay didn't live too far from me, so I jumped back in my car and was pulling up to her crib within minutes.

Settling in, I took a nice hot shower and handled my hygiene. My day was long and aggravating dealing with the guys. All I wanted was some chill time with my girl, some food, and drinks to go with it.

Once I was dressed, I made my way downstairs and saw Angela had already arrived.

"Took you long enough," she joked, already with a drink in her hand.

"Damn, you couldn't wait?" I cracked back.

"Nope, but here's yours." She handed me a glass of wine.

Shanay was in the kitchen finishing up dinner while Ang and I were in the living room chopping it up. I had planned on drinking until I couldn't feel anything. The following day I had off from work, so I didn't need to worry about potentially dragging myself to work hungover.

"Oh, I made that call, and my people pushed it through. She should be gone within the next week or so. It's transport every Monday on the airlift in Harrisburg," Ang informed me.

The night started off great, I thought.

"Good looking on that."

"Anything for you." We toasted glasses.

Shanay walked in with our plates of shrimp alfredo. The aroma filled the room, making my stomach growl. I couldn't wait another second. I dug right in and started to devour my food.

After a few minutes of silence between us all, with only the music being heard, we finished up our meal.

"That shit was so good, Nay. Thank you," I sang happily.

My belly was full, I was sipping on some nice wine, and I was with my girls. I couldn't have asked for a better night.

"Your food almost made me have an orgasm," Angela joked. "But it couldn't beat the real thing my boo be giving me."

"What boo?" Shanay jumped up and asked.

"Right, what boo?" I eyed her.

"Ughhh. Oh, my God. Alright. I've been fucking around with this guy from my job. I like him too, and the sex, baby, the sex is everything."

"Wait, do I know him?" I raised a brow.

"I believe you do, well, you should. You're his superior."

"Who bitch?"

"Curtis," she blurted out.

Fuck, I thought. The glass in my hand slipped out of my grasp and crashed onto the floor, shattering into pieces.

"Tiffany, you okay?" Shanay rushed over to me.

I was just staring at Ang while images of me and Curt flicked through my mind.

"What's wrong?" Angela asked suspiciously.

I contemplated on whether to tell her the truth or to keep me and Curt's dealings to myself. After the argument I had with him earlier that day, I wasn't sure if keeping it from her was smart. Curt could've easily told her. Then, I would be the one looking shady as fuck for not letting her know.

"Ummm, Ang. Curt and I have been dealing, too."

"Oh fuck," Shanay blurted out while cleaning up the mess I made.

"Cap! You're joking, right?" Ang asked with uncertainty in her voice.

"I wish I was. I had no idea that y'all was talking. I'm—"

"Just stop, Tiffany. It's like you just can't leave any men for anyone else. You've always been like this." She stood to her feet. "You worried about getting dicked down by someone, you need to focus on your marriage and why your husband ain't been throwing pipe your way." She grabbed her bag and phone. "Shanay, I'm out. I'll call you later."

Storming out of the house, she slammed the door shut, making me jump. In one day, I got into it with three different people. I was feeling like the dirt under someone's shoe, the way each one spoke to me. For a moment, I had to stop and think. Was it because of me that everything was backfiring, or was it just a fucked-up coincidence? Either way, something had to give.

"You okay?" Shanay asked.

I didn't know how to answer that question, so I just did what I was longing to do: cry.

Chapter 6

After having two days off from work, I was somewhat rejuvenated and ready to get back. Since I started being active again after so long, it was hard to stay stagnant for too long. On my off days, I was ready to go in just to stay busy. I even picked up doubles that allowed me to have a long break in between. Besides, it was the perfect distraction from life in general.

I had to handle some business for Manic, and once it was done, I wanted to see him. We hadn't spoken or saw each other since the little rift we had; he only sent messages through some of the COs on his team. At the end of the day, I knew I still held a valuable part in his operation, so he couldn't have gotten rid of me that easy.

Once the last count was completed and clear, I kicked back

in my office for a few hours to get my mind right before approaching Manic. I didn't know what type of timing he was on, so I mentally prepared myself for anything and prayed for a good outcome.

Finally, I started my rounds around the building, leaving five-south last. I picked that particular night to go and see him because I scheduled Wright to be the overnight guard for their unit. When I got inside, I sent for Manic, then went straight inside the kitchen and patiently waited for him to come. It took longer than usual, which had me worried that he wasn't going to show due to how I acted.

When the door opened and I saw it was him, my heart skipped a beat. I missed his face and his whole entire being for that matter.

"What you want?" he asked as soon as he saw me.

"Damn, it's like that?" I retorted, leaning up against the metal counter.

"I'm tired. Wassup Tiffany?"

Remembering I was in the wrong and wanted to make things right, I remained humble and responded properly.

"Manic, I'm sorry about the line of questioning. I got carried away, and that was my fault. Would you forgive me?"

He looked at me with hooded eyes. "You sure you won't be on no more bullshit?" He squinted.

In my head, Briana was going to be out of the building any day, so I had no worries. "I'm positive," I assured him.

"Ard. One more time to be on some dumb shit and I'm good on you."

"I got it. Now, can I start making up for it?" I asked seductively.

He chuckled as he shot me a grin.

"How you gon do that?" He leaned up against the wall.

"I can show you better than I can tell you." I walked up to him and pulled down his shorts and boxers.

His dick wasn't hard like it usually would've been. I paid it no mind because I knew he wasn't feeling me until moments before. And, yet, he probably was still iffy.

Putting the whole stick in my mouth, it fit because he wasn't erect yet. Within a few moments and a number of strokes and sucks later, he was up and active. I missed his scent and how he tasted. I devoured his dick as if it was going to be my last supper. By his reaction, I knew he was into it.

"Shit, Tiff. Let me fuck your face."

I looked up at him and nodded.

Standing upward, Manic palmed my head with both hands and drove his dick in and out of my mouth like it was my pussy he was fucking. With every thrust, I felt the head of his tool touching the little thingy thing in the back of my throat. My eyes watered from the forceful penetration, and there were times I gagged, but never let up.

Leaning my head upwards a little, he continued his attack on my mouth as he looked down at me. Randomly, he pulled his dick out and told me to open my mouth. He spit in my mouth, then shoved his dick right back in it.

"Fuck," he groaned.

After another minute, he pulled out again, but that time he placed a condom on, which prompted me to get up and drop my pants.

Spinning me around, he bent me over and rammed his dick inside of me without warning. Manic grabbed a fistful of hair and tugged at it so that my back was arched. He slapped my ass hard a few times, making a loud noise. I was on cloud nine at the time, so I didn't give a fuck who heard us.

Manic pumped in and out and in and out without mercy. It almost felt like he was fucking me extra hard to punish me for doing something bad. I started to run just a little, but I couldn't go anywhere; I was tied up in his grip.

"Don't run. This is what you wanted, right? Take this dick," he growled.

"Mmmhmm," I whimpered as I took all his inches and bangs.

In my head, I thought there was no way in hell he could fuck me the way he did and not have any feelings. I thought I was playing a dangerous game dealing with him, but instead, he was the one playing a dangerous game.

Palming my chin from the back with both hands, he dipped and thrust upwards inside me, hitting my spot. His pace sped up, and before I knew it, he was exploding inside the condom, still inside of me.

"Shiiittt," he hissed out of breath. "I missed that shit." He palmed and slapped me on the ass.

"I missed y'all, too," I told him, referring to him and his dick.

We got ourselves together, and before he left out, I remembered I had something important to tell him.

"We may have a problem," I blurted out.

"What kind of problem?" His eyebrows knitted.

"Curt found out about us and threatened to tell it all," I informed him.

"Goofy ass nigga, man." He shook his head. "That was yo nigga or something?"

"No, we just fooled around."

"And that nigga in his feelings like that over some pussy? He must've forgotten who got him living real fuckin' nice outside."

"We gotta talk—"

"Talk? I don't do no talking shorty unless it's negotiating numbers. I'll handle his ass, don't worry," he assured me.

I wasn't sure what Manic had up his sleeve to deal with Curt, but I didn't care. Making threats like that was serious, and he had to be held accountable for his actions.

Better him than me, I thought.

"So, you want the house, that's it?" my lawyer asked me.

I stopped playing around and finally hired a divorce attorney to handle my situation with Rich. Going through everything with him only made me stronger. I grew a backbone and wasn't tolerating any more bullshit from him, or anyone else for that matter.

"Yes, nothing more, nothing less," I confirmed.

She nodded and jotted down notes in her book. "That shouldn't be a problem. I know you said you didn't want anything else, but I will make sure you get what you deserve."

It felt good to hear someone was going to defend and fight for me because I was usually the one doing all the fighting.

We wrapped up our meeting, and I made my way over to the house to grab some paperwork my lawyer requested. If it wasn't urgent, I would send her copies of them; I would've prolonged going to the house.

When I got there, I saw Rich's car parked out front. I started to pull right off and come back another time, but then, remembered I had heat in my bag. Checking in my purse, I grabbed my nine-millimeter and double-checked the clip. Making sure the safety was still on, I placed it in the waistband on my back. I climbed out of the car and made my way inside the house. Of course, Rich was right there in the living room on the game. When he saw me, he looked like he saw a ghost.

I swiftly climbed the stairs to our bedroom and went into my document drawer to retrieve what I had gone there for.

Moments later, I heard footsteps coming my way. When I turned, it was Rich.

"So, you out in the streets acting like you're not married?" he asked sarcastically.

"Married?" I chuckled. "Rich, leave me alone."

"Tiffany, I'm sorry baby," he made his way over to me and pleaded.

"I know you are, and it's okay." I smiled.

I walked off, leaving him standing there looking dumbfounded. By the time I made it back downstairs, he was hot on my ass. Grabbing my forearm, he tried to pull me towards him. I reached for my nine and pulled it out on him. He quickly lifted his hands in the air.

"I said leave me the fuck alone, Richard," I gritted.

"Yeah, your hoe ass done lost your goofy ass mind. Get the fuck out, Tiffany."

"Glady." I lowered the gun and dashed out of the crib.

Once back in my car, I let out a deep breath. I was playing hardball, but that was an intense move I made against him. Rich wasn't a pussy nigga; I was just happy things didn't go south.

Pulling off in the direction of FDC Philly, I bumped my music and allowed my thoughts to run on Manic. He had been on my mind lately. Things were almost back to normal with us after we resolved our issues a week before. Business was running smoothly, and we were back fucking the shit out of each other.

When I reached work, Angela and I ended up on the same elevator going up. We didn't say a word to one another. The tension was thick as hell, and I hated that for us. She was one of my best friends, and the fact a nigga was able to come between us made me upset. I wanted so badly to say something, but I left it alone. The workplace wasn't the right space or time to try to hash out our issues.

As I was unlocking my office door, I felt someone come up behind me, so I quickly turned around to see Angela standing there with a sad face.

"Can we talk?" she asked.

I nodded and proceeded to enter my office with her in tow. "Wassup?" I asked as I rested my belongings and took a seat.

"Tiffany, I'm sorry for acting the way I did and for saying all those hurtful things. I was drawn for real. I hope you can forgive me, so we can move past this," she expressed.

I didn't think I was going to see the day I would get an apology from Angela "Miss Always Right" Cummings. It made me feel good though, to know I wasn't in the wrong. We both had no clue we were dealing with him at the same time. That's what we got for trying to keep our niggas on the hush tip.

"I forgive you, girl. Let it be the first and last nigga that comes between us. He wasn't even all that anyway," I joked.

"True, and you wouldn't believe what happened."

"What?" I raised a brow.

"He got caught fucking one of the female inmates and got a PREA charge," she exclaimed.

"Get the fuck out of here. You serious?" My mouth dropped wide open.

Manic, I thought.

"So serious. When I found out, I wanted to throw up. I couldn't believe he was the reason we stopped talking. I don't care if it wasn't for that long but still."

"Fuck him and fuck that situation. It's in the past," I told her. "Come, give me a hug."

We stood up and embraced each other with a sisterly hug. Making up with Angela made my day, but finding out Manic stood on business and handled Curt made me even happier. Everything was slowly falling into place.

"Oh yeah, your girl is out of here today," Ang informed me.

"Who, Briana?" My eyes grew wide.

"Yup."

I almost jumped out of my skin. A big smile graced my face, knowing she was about to be gone. Just when I thought my day couldn't get any better, another problem was solved. There was only one other thing left on my list to be resolved, and I knew that was going to take some time. But the fact that I started the process of getting divorced was a huge step in the right direction, so that made me feel good.

My prayers did get answered, along with work being put in. I wasn't sure what my future had in store for me. All I knew was that everything I wanted, I was going to get, and whatever I had, I was going to fight to keep, if it was worth it. I was no longer the silly weak bitch; I was that bitch. A force to be reckoned with.

Did you enjoy the read?
Let us know how much by leaving us a review on Amazon and Goodreads.

Keep reading for a preview of…

Wet Dreams on Lockdown: The Unit Manager
By Nai

CHAPTER 1

Camille

I moaned and panted, thrashing my face from side to side as my lover took complete control of my body with the flick of his tongue. He'd swiped it up and down my slit, stopping at my clit, giving it a light suck, before inserting two fingers inside my love cave. I was so wet and couldn't recall a time I'd experienced this kind of ecstasy. My eyelids became heavy, making it hard to keep my eyes open as and my clit swelled twice its size, and my orgasm grew.

"Mmmhmm, gimmie that shit, baby," he nastily encouraged, adding more pressure, eagerly anticipating the juices that were sure to pour out of me, and onto his awaiting tongue.

His encouragement was music to my ears as I lifted my

right breast and used my long tongue to graze my nipple. "Ooouu, shit, you gon' make me cum," I announced, breathless, grinding my fat pussy in his mouth. He responded by lifting my waist off the bed and sliding his finger into my ass. "Oh, my godddd, what are you doing to me?!" My eyes rolled in the back of my head as my legs shook. "Ooouu, I'm cummin'!!!" The floodgates opened and I squirted, wetting his face up.

"Good girl, Mama." He gave my pussy a light slap before placing me flat on the bed again. Kissing my inner thighs, he made a trail up my body, stopping at my mouth.

Using his tongue to part my full lips, we engaged in the most passionate French kiss. The feeling of him running his dick up and down my slit was heavenly. I fought the urge to guide him into me but remembering his demand to let him have his way with me, I waited anxiously for what was to come. As he slid into me inch by inch, my mouth fell agape, speaking the only audible words that came to mind. "I love you."

"I love you, too," I heard back, and my eyes popped open. Turning my head, I found my boyfriend of a year staring back at me with a goofy smile plastered on his face. "I was tearing that pussy up in yo dream, wasn't I?" Omar thrust his hips upward, playfully humping the air.

"Huh?" I questioned, dumbfounded, with a hint of disappointment laced in my tone that couldn't be missed.

"In yo' dream, bae. You've been moaning and shit for the

past eight minutes. I was tempted to put this dick on you, but a nigga just got in from working a double and I know I wouldn't have lasted long." He chuckled like there was a comical line in his statement.

I didn't find his truth funny at all. Not one to crush my man's ego, I gave him a lazy smile and pecked his lips. "Yeah, you were doin' yo shit, bae. I gotta go shower."

Standing up, I felt the wetness from my sex running down my legs. Having slept naked, the silhouette of my voluptuous 183lbs was visible on the wall as I walked around the bed, in the dimly lit room.

"Damn, baby, you left a puddle on your side," Omar let out. He wasn't telling me anything that I didn't already know. When rubbed the right way, this super soaker had a mind of her own.

"It be like that sometimes," was all I could say as I left the room to shower in the hallway bathroom.

There was a bathroom in my bedroom that I could've used but I needed to come down off my sex high in peace. I didn't want to have to think about the man's feelings on the other side of the door, my man. I'd gotten caught up in another wet dream. This one being more intense than the last. The six foot four, peanut butter skin toned, furry browed, brown-eyed, no-nonsense Cameron had invaded my home and made his way into my dreams once again. I couldn't shake his fine ass.

"Get it together, Cam," I spoke to myself in the mirror. *"Don't make no damn sense lusting over no man like that. And*

you," I cast my eyes downward to address my kitty. *"You need to get a grip. Well... I mean, your grip isn't the issue...but, you know what I mean. Behave."* Giving my phat ma a light smack, my clit responded. Throwing my head back, I bit my lip. I was such a damn freak.

Shaking my head, I leaned over and turned on the shower. While I felt wrong for having secret sex that had been reserved for my dreams over the last six months, it was only through those dreams that I was able to reach my orgasmic peak. Omar couldn't keep up with my sex drive, nor keep my salacious sexual appetite fed. I wanted every inch of my body explored. I wanted a nigga to sign his name on this pussy. And though I wanted Omar to be the man for the job, at 31 years young, I couldn't see myself teaching any man how to please me.

Often, I found myself wondering if the mediocre sex was enough to chuck the deuces on him but always talked myself out of calling it quits. I was strongly opposed to going through the whole *getting to know you* phase with anyone else. I'd given Omar a hard enough time in the beginning of our relationship, so in a way, I felt obligated to see it through. We met in a small coffee shop a year ago and I was just twenty-four hours fresh off a breakup. I'd spent the previous night packing up my ex-boyfriend of five years belongings after deciding I was tired of housing a bum with good dick and no ambition.

It was crazy how I let good dick cloud my judgment for that long, but it was a lesson learned. While Omar's smile was genuine and his pick-up lines unique, I wasn't going for it and shut down his request for my number as soon as it passed his lips. Seeing him a few more times at the coffee shop after that, his persistence eventually wore me down. After two months of courting, we began dating exclusively. Once it was solidified, I put the pussy on him that night. And that night, I found out that the dick wasn't hittin' on shit.

Still, I put my need for mind-blowing sex to the side. Even if I had to find other ways to get myself off. Wet dreams and keeping my rose in my nightstand as well as my purse in case I ever felt the need to take the edge off had become a thing. Now, I was far from a nympho, but sex for me was just as important in a relationship as communication. And that may sound crazy, considering I couldn't communicate to my man that his sex was a three and a half on a one to ten scale. Sighing, I hopped in the shower and washed myself from head to toe twice before stepping out and into my towel.

Drying off, I wrapped the towel tightly around my body and went back to the room. Thankfully, Omar was fast asleep. I didn't want him to see me leave the room after slipping on my panties and a T-shirt. He was a cuddler and I didn't feel right cuddling up with him after the dream I'd had. I also didn't enjoy sleeping in the wet spot.

Grabbing my phone and tumbler filled with ice water from the nightstand, I quietly crept out and made my way to the living room. I had a good two hours before I had to get up and get ready for work. Unfolding the Ugg throw blanket that lay across the couch, I covered myself up with it and closed my eyes. Sleep came easy, as it often did after a good orgasm. And though I felt wrong for having them, I had to admit that the wet dreams were good for the body.

***

"Okay, and what did you do after that?" My best friend, Janell asked as we caught up on our morning FaceTime call while I drove to work.

"After my shower, I threw some clothes on and went to the living room to sleep."

"Bitch, you did what?!" She jumped up from her desk, knocking her chair over. She was as dramatic as she was loyal. **"Hold on, lemme close this door before my students come in."**

Janell was a sixth-grade ELA teacher at a Charter school. One would have never known that the Howard University grad had such a foul mouth and a thing for women by the way she carried herself. I knew, though. We had been best friends since high school and inseparable. People often speculated about us bumping coochies because it was rare that you saw me without her and vice versa. It didn't help that she was open about her love for the female anatomy. But still, I didn't let the rumors bother me. Janell was my ace.

"Yeah, or the principal."

"Girl, ain't nobody scared of that old white lady. Any who, please tell me why you thought it was okay to fall into a peaceful slumber, on the couch after being fucked by another man in your dreams."

"What else would you have had me do that would've made more sense, Nell?"

"Fuck him, Camille. You were supposed to fuck yo' man and any doubt that may have crept into his mind."

"Didn't I tell you he thought it was him in the dream?"

"All the more reason to have fucked the shit out of him so the thought remained." She sighed. **"You being friends with me this long and actin' like you don't know how to think ahead is rather appalling."**

"Girl shut up, wasn't nobody doing all that. He was asleep once I was out of the shower. Back to the reason I called, though. The dreams are becoming more frequent and I'm about to lose my damn mind. This gotta be some kind of sign."

The school bell could be heard in the background, signaling the end of our conversation.

"Drinks and dinner at my house later?"

"I'd love to, babes. And I'm spending the night."

"So, you can wet up my sheets, I think not." She put her hand up to her mouth to hide her laugh.

"I would call you out your name, but I'm gonna save it for later. Have a great day, heaux."

"And you have a splendid one, Ms. Wet Wet." She blew me a kiss and disconnected the call.

Pulling into the employee parking lot of Fishkill Correctional Facility, I parked in my assigned spot. Taking the keys out of the ignition, I put my iPad in my purse and grabbed my tea. As the Unit Manager at the all-male facility, I was responsible for conducting daily rounds of my unit to pinpoint security breaches, reviewing inmate behavior logs, etc. to ensure compliance with the facility. I'd worked at the prison for four years and had just entered my second year in the position. Moving up in the ranks so quickly wasn't a surprise, seeing as I had all the great qualities of a leader.

It also helped that the inmates in my unit rocked with me heavily. I'd been assigned to what the inmates called a "thunder dorm". Things could pop off at any given time and they had, but once I was put in position, the unit had done a 180. Not only did I give the guys the same respect as I gave anyone on the outside, but I gave them something to look at. Standing at five foot six, I was a thick woman.

From my ample breasts to the pudge around my stomach, down to my thick hips and round ass, the men awaited my walkthrough Monday through Friday. With a round face, my eyes, nose, and chin were perfectly proportioned. My skin tone mirrored the color of Jack Daniels liquor, and my face had a permanent glow due to my daily skincare routine. I loved my job, interacting with the people that society had cast away on some levels. Though I had a few battles here and there with the men who wanted to throw their weight around, the good outweighed the bad for the most part.

Using my badge, I entered Unit H and greeted the officers who'd worked the overnight shift and went straight to my office. Setting my bag down, I powered up my computer to check my emails and to-do list for the day. There was so much to be done over the span of eight hours, but I made sure to never leave work left over for the next day.

I prided myself on being efficient and it showed every time I went up for review with the warden. Grabbing my blinged-out clipboard, I walked out onto the compound to do my daily walkthrough. Typically, the men would be out of their cells, moving about freely, but they'd been on lockdown for the last week due to an altercation that resulted in a stabbing. I hated to make everyone pay for the actions of two individuals, but rules were rules, and there was but so much leeway I could give. My first stop was the control room.

"Hey, Dave. How were my men last night?" I asked one of the officers who often had issues in the unit because of his attitude.

"Quiet for the most part but you know there's always a select few that want to act an ass to prove something to the rest of the lowlifes."

My face formed a small smile as I asked for the names of the inmates he was referring to so I could jot them down. I wasn't smiling because I agreed with his statement, but I had mastered the art of killing people with kindness. He read off a list of four names and I nodded. "Thanks." Turning to leave, I paused to address him again. "You know, if you weren't so aggressive in your approach, maybe you'd have a different result. Yes, we want to be stern, but when it gets to being a dick-swinging contest, that's where we fall short."

Dave gave a nod of contempt, followed by a forced smile. "I'll keep that in mind."

"Sounds good." I was good for having the last word.

Leaving the control room, I headed back out to start my rounds and speak with the guys Dave mentioned.

"Aye, Ms. D, I need to holla atchu' for a second."

"Ms. D, they need to fix the heat in here."

"You looking good today, Ms. D."

"Ms. D, they didn't take my sto' sheet yesterday."

As I went to each cell, there was a different request, grievance, or some kind of compliment being thrown at me. I spoke to everyone, making sure to write down every issue, even if I felt it was ridiculous or an outright lie. Once I'd gone through the top tier, I did the same with the bottom. Reaching the last cell, I took a deep breath before calling out to the inmate. He was the last person Dave had named on his list and one that stayed to himself for the most part.

He was transferred to the facility six months ago and it didn't take long for him to learn the ropes and establish himself. He was a loner for sure, but the inmates seemed to gravitate to him. Respectful, he demanded respect in return from inmates and staff alike.

"Haynes," I called out to him, and he appeared at the window a few seconds later. "How's it going?"

"Why do you insist on calling me, Haynes?" His authoritative yet sexy tone made me suck in a breath. Taking in his almond-colored skin, perfectly chiseled jawline, suckable lips, and alluring eyes, I unconsciously shifted from side to side, feeling my nipples harden.

Gathering myself, I hid my true feelings behind a professional smile. "I call you by your last name like everyone else here."

"I ain't everyone else in here, though. I'm Cameron." He rubbed his low-cut fade and his lips curled into a small smile.

His name sounded even better coming from him than the times I'd cried it out during one of my toe-curling orgasms. He was Cameron Haynes; the inmate that had hijacked my inner thoughts and dreams.

Available now on all platforms!

ALSO BY P. WISE

Bound to a Savage

Melted the Heart of a Menace

My Curves Captivated a Hood Millionaire: A BBW Love Story

My Curves Captivated a Hood Millionaire: A BBW Love Story 2

Come Play In It: An Urban Erotica

Heir to the Plug's Throne

Heir to the Plug's Throne 2

Gorgeous Gangstas

Gorgeous Gangstas 2

Gorgeous Gangstas 3

Luchiano Mob Ties: Snatched Up by a Don Spin-Off

Snatched Up by a Don: A BBW Love Story

Snatched Up by a Don: A BBW Love Story 2

Snatched Up by a Don: A BBW Love Story 3

A Saint Luv'n A Savage: A Philly Love Story

Luv'n a Philly Boss: A Saint Luv'n a Savage Spin-off

Kwon: Clone of a Savage

Kwon: Clone of a Savage 2

Welcome to Cherrieville: Bitter & Sweet

Summer Luvin' with a NY Baller

Tamia & Tytus: A Toxic Love Affair

Diary of a Brooklyn Girl

Sex, Scams, & Brisks

Sex, Scams, & Brisks 2

OTHER BOOKS BY

URBAN AINT DEAD

Tales 4rm Da Dale

The Hottest Summer Ever

Hittin' Licks For The Holidays: Atlanta

Wet Dreams On Lockdown: The Nurse

By **Elijah R. Freeman**

Despite The Odds

By **Juhnell Morgan**

Good Girl Gone Rogue

By **Manny Black**

Hittaz

Hittaz 2

Hittaz 3

Hittaz 4

Coldhearted

By **Lou Garden Price, Sr.**

Charge It To The Game

Charge It To The Game 2

A Summer To Remember With My Hitta

Snatched Up By A Hitta

Santa Sent Me A Real One For Christmas

Wet Dreams on Lockdown: The Unit Manager

By **Nai**

A Setup For Revenge

Wet Dreams On Lockdown: The Librarian

By **Ashley Williams**

Ridin' For You

Trickin' on a Heaux for Christmas: A BBW Love Story

Homie Hoppin' For The Holidays

Wet Dreams on Lockdown: The Female C.O

By **Telia Teanna**

The State's Witness

The State's Witness 2

The State's Witness 3

By **Kyiris Ashley**

Stuck In The Trenches

Stuck In The Trenches 2

By **Huff Tha Great**

The Swipe

By **Toōla**

Melted the Heart of a Menace

By P. Wise

Merry Trapmas: Ice & Frost

By **Mia Sky**

Thug Me The Right Way

By **DiamondATL & Nai**

Wet Dreams on Lockdown: The Male C.O

By **Tamyra Griffin**

Wet Dreams On Lockdown: The Counselor

By **Paris Iman**

Wet Dreams On Lockdown: The Warden

By **Shawnice**

Wet Dreams On Lockdown: The Captain

By **TN Jones**

Coming Soon From
<u>URBAN AINT DEAD</u>

The Hottest Summer Ever 2
THE G-CODE
How To Publish A Book From Prison
Tales 4rm Da Dale 2
By **Elijah R. Freeman**

Hittaz 5
Coldhearted 2
By **Lou Garden Price, Sr.**

The Swipe 2
By **Toola**

Good Girls Gone Rogue 2
By **Manny Black**

Despite The Odds 2
Hittin' Licks For The Holidays: Chicago
By **Juhnell Morgan**

Charge It To The Game 3
By **Nai**

Ridin For You, Too
By **Telia Teanna**

A Setup For Revenge 2
By **Ashley Williams**

A Gangsta's Last Kiss
By **Mia Sky**

Pretti & The Beast
By **P. Wise**

BOOKS BY

URBAN AINT DEAD's C.E.O

<u>Elijah R. Freeman</u>

Triggadale

Triggadale 2

Triggadale 3

Tales 4rm Da Dale

The Hottest Summer Ever

Murda Was The Case

Murda Was The Case 2

Murda Was The Case 3

Hittin' Licks For The Holidays: Atlanta

Wet Dreams On Lockdown: The Nurse

www.ingramcontent.com/pod-product-compliance
Lightning Source LLC
Chambersburg PA
CBHW071200300726
48975CB00004B/1226